10 Trick-or-Treaters

A Halloween Counting Book

by **Janet Schulman** • illustrated by **Linda Davick**

Alfred A. Knopf

New York

10 trick-or-treaters
on a dark and spooky night
out to get some candy
or give someone a fright.

10 trick-or-treaters . . .

standing in a line.
Along came a spider . . .

and then there were 9.

9 trick-or-treaters,
the night was getting late.
A toad hopped near . . .

and then there were 8.

8 trick-or-treaters
under racing clouds in heaven.
A bat flew by . . .

and then there were 7.

7 trick-or-treaters
filling sacks with party mix.
A ghost said,
"Boo!" . . . .

and then there were 6.

6 trick-or-treaters
dancing to some jive.
A skeleton tried
to join them . . .

and then there were 5.

5 trick-or-treaters
knocking on a door.
"Who's there?"
called a witch . . .

and then there were 4.

4 trick-or-treaters
counting candy by a tree.
A monster cried,
"Gimme some!" . . .

and then there were 3.

3 trick-or-treaters—
why are there so few?
A vampire crooned,
"Good evening" . . .

and then there were 2.

2 trick-or-treaters,
they've had a night of fun.
A mummy stumbled by them . . .

and then there was 1.

1 brave trick-or-treater,
her Halloween is done.
She climbed into bed . . .

and then
there were
none.

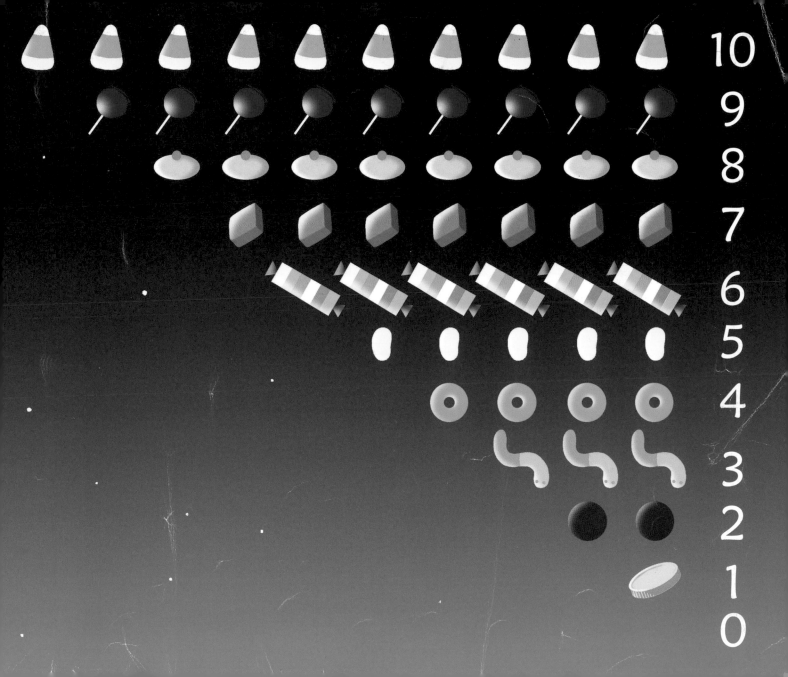

For Erin Clarke
—J.S.

For Princess Aggles
—L.D.

THIS IS A BORZOI BOOK PUBLISHED BY ALFRED A. KNOPF
Text copyright © 2005 by Janet Schulman
Illustrations copyright © 2005 by Linda Davick
All rights reserved under International and Pan-American Copyright Conventions. Published in the United States by
Alfred A. Knopf, an imprint of Random House Children's Books, a division of Random House, Inc., New York,
and simultaneously in Canada by Random House of Canada Limited, Toronto.
Distributed by Random House, Inc., New York.
KNOPF, BORZOI BOOKS, and the colophon are registered trademarks of Random House, Inc.
www.randomhouse.com/kids

Library of Congress Cataloging-in-Publication Data
Schulman, Janet.
10 trick-or-treaters : a Halloween counting book / by Janet Schulman ; illustrated by Linda Davick. — 1st ed.
p.   cm.
SUMMARY: Ten trick-or-treaters start out on Halloween night, but they disappear one by one as they encounter
a spider, a vampire, a ghost, and other scary creatures.
ISBN 0-375-83225-4 (trade) — ISBN 0-375-93225-9 (lib. bdg.)
[1. Halloween—Fiction. 2. Counting. 3. Stories in rhyme.] I. Title: Ten trick-or-treaters. II. Davick, Linda, ill. III. Title.
PZ8.3.S29737Aae 2005
[E]—dc22
2004010831

MANUFACTURED IN MALAYSIA
August 2005
10 9 8 7 6 5 4 3 2 1
First Edition